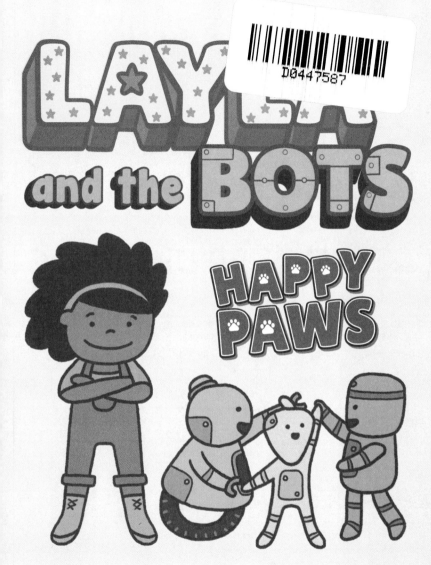

LAYLA and the BOTS

HAPPY PAWS

written by
Vicky Fang

illustrated by
Christine Nishiyama

BRANCHES

SCHOLASTIC INC.

For my rock stars, Taso & Leo –VF
To Declan. For everything. –CN

Text copyright © 2020 by Vicky Fang
Illustrations copyright © 2020 by Christine Nishiyama

All rights reserved. Published by Scholastic Inc., *Publishers since 1920.* SCHOLASTIC, BRANCHES, and associated logos are trademarks and/or registered trademarks of Scholastic Inc.

The publisher does not have any control over and does not assume any responsibility for author or third-party websites or their content.

No part of this publication may be reproduced, stored in a retrieval system, or transmitted in any form or by any means, electronic, mechanical, photocopying, recording, or otherwise, without written permission of the publisher. For information regarding permission, write to Scholastic Inc., Attention: Permissions Department, 557 Broadway, New York, NY 10012.

This book is a work of fiction. Names, characters, places, and incidents are either the product of the author's imagination or are used fictitiously, and any resemblance to actual persons, living or dead, business establishments, events, or locales is entirely coincidental.

ISBN 978-1-338-84588-4

10 9 8 7 6 5 4 3 2 1   22 23 24 25 26

Printed in the U.S.A. 40
This edition first printing April 2022

Illustrated by Christine Nishiyama
Edited by Rachel Matson and Katie Carella
Book design by Maria Mercado

TABLE OF CONTENTS

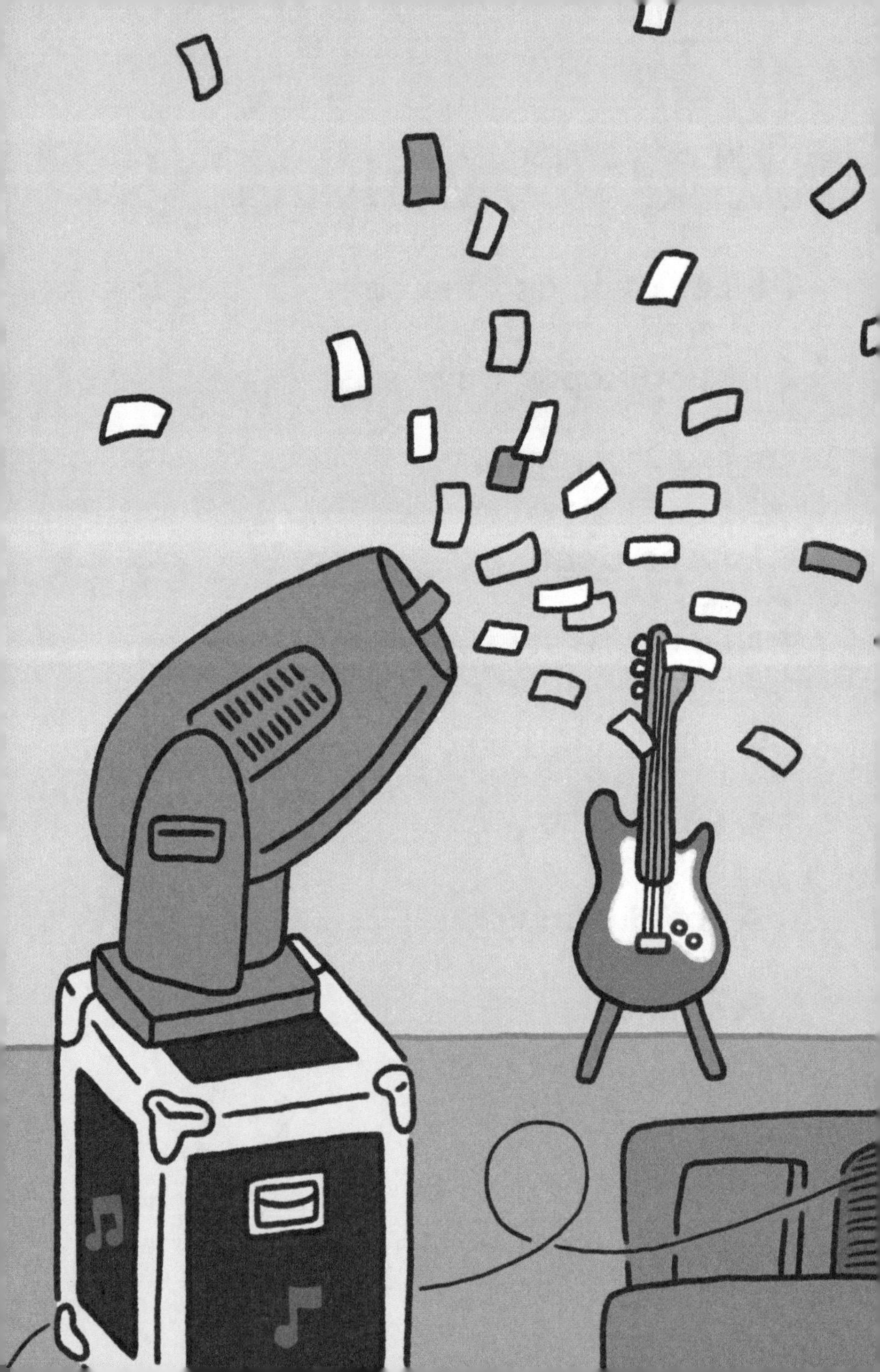

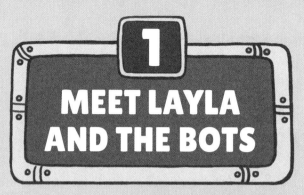

1
MEET LAYLA AND THE BOTS

This is Layla. She is an inventor. And a rock star.

These are the Bots.

They are part of Layla's crew.

Beep knows things.

BEEP.
Light travels faster than anything else in this world!

Boop builds things.

More lights?

Bop codes things.

```
on [POSE] -> lights!
lights {brightness = 100;
color = rainbow_dazzle;
pattern = Super _____;
duration =              240 seconds;}
```

Ready-yah!

Layla and the Bots live in an ordinary town called Blossom Valley.

But ever since Layla built her Bots, her life is anything but ordinary.

You see, Layla and the Bots are famous!
They play awesome rock music together
and perform in all sorts of cool places.

And when they're
not playing music,
they're putting their
invention skills to work.

Whenever Layla and the Bots get together, awesome things happen.

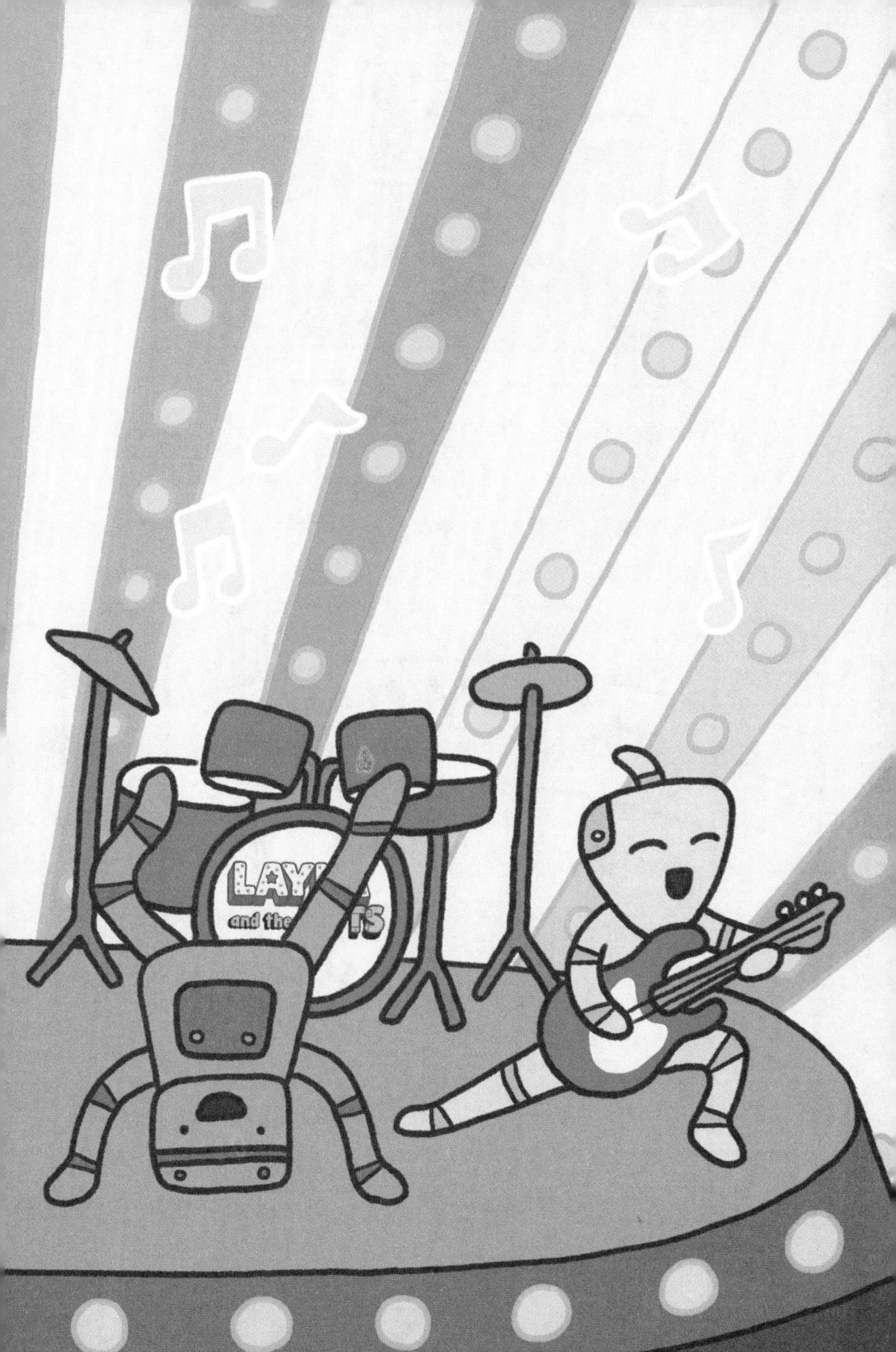

2
NOT-SO-HAPPY DAYS

On Monday morning, Layla and the Bots unpack their band gear at the Happy Days Amusement Park. They have a big show in five days!

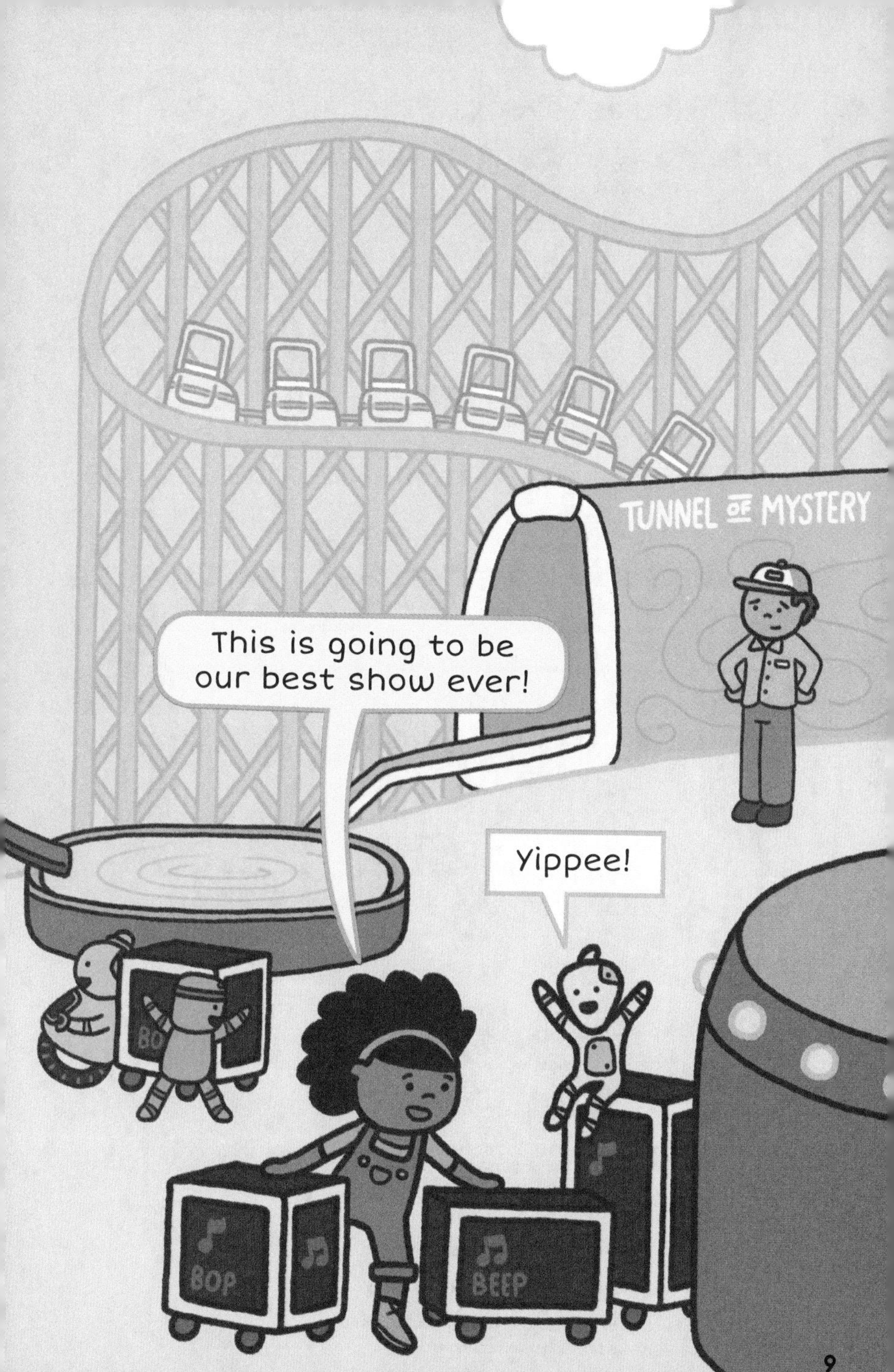
TUNNEL OF MYSTERY
This is going to be our best show ever!
Yippee!
BO
BOP
BEEP

Layla sees Wade, the park owner. He looks upset.

She hops down from the stage.

Hey, Wade. Is everything okay?

Sorry, but your show is canceled. I am closing the park.

What? But why?

People have stopped coming to the park. It's been slow for a year. I just can't stay open.

Wade seems so sad. He keeps talking, but Layla doesn't hear him. Close Happy Days? She has so many memories from the park!

After Wade leaves, Layla tells the Bots the bad news.

Wade is closing Happy Days!

How come?

Warghh!

BEEP. Happy Days is my favorite—

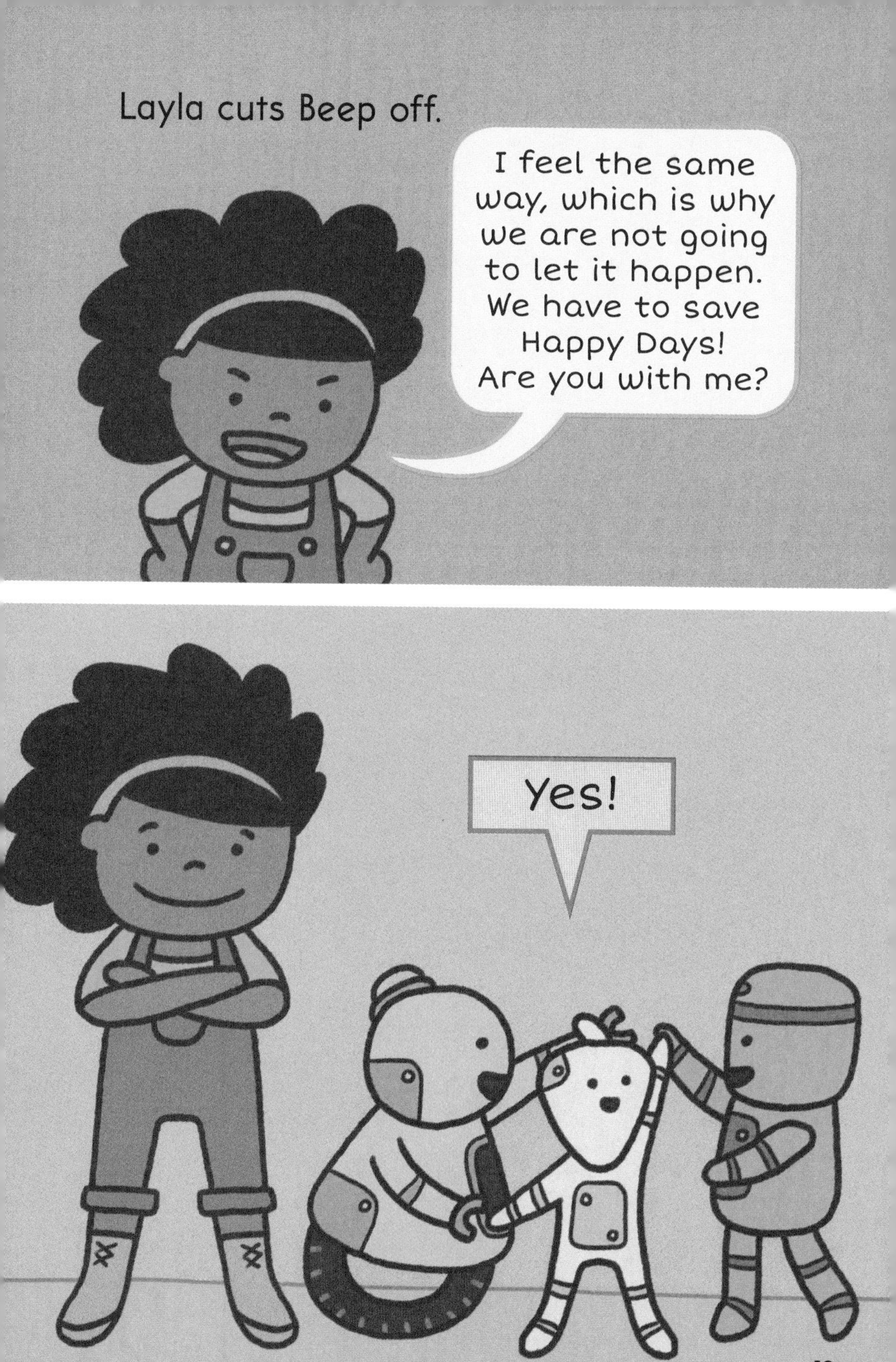
Layla cuts Beep off.
I feel the same way, which is why we are not going to let it happen. We have to save Happy Days! Are you with me?
Yes!

3
FOLLOW THAT BARK

Layla and the Bots visit town.

It's time to investigate. We have to figure out why people have stopped going to Happy Days. Where are they going instead?

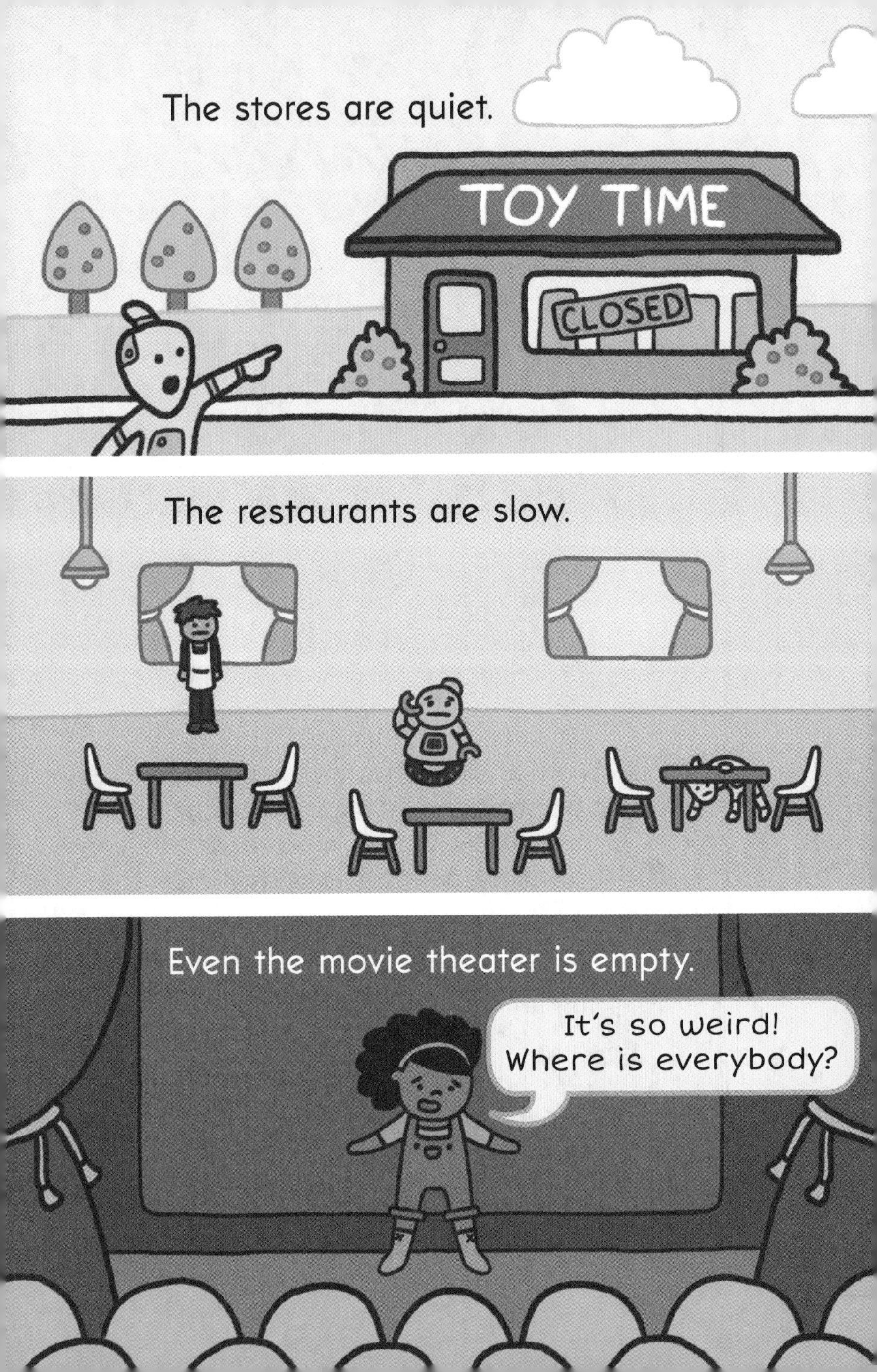
The stores are quiet.
TOY TIME
CLOSED
The restaurants are slow.
Even the movie theater is empty.
It's so weird!
Where is everybody?

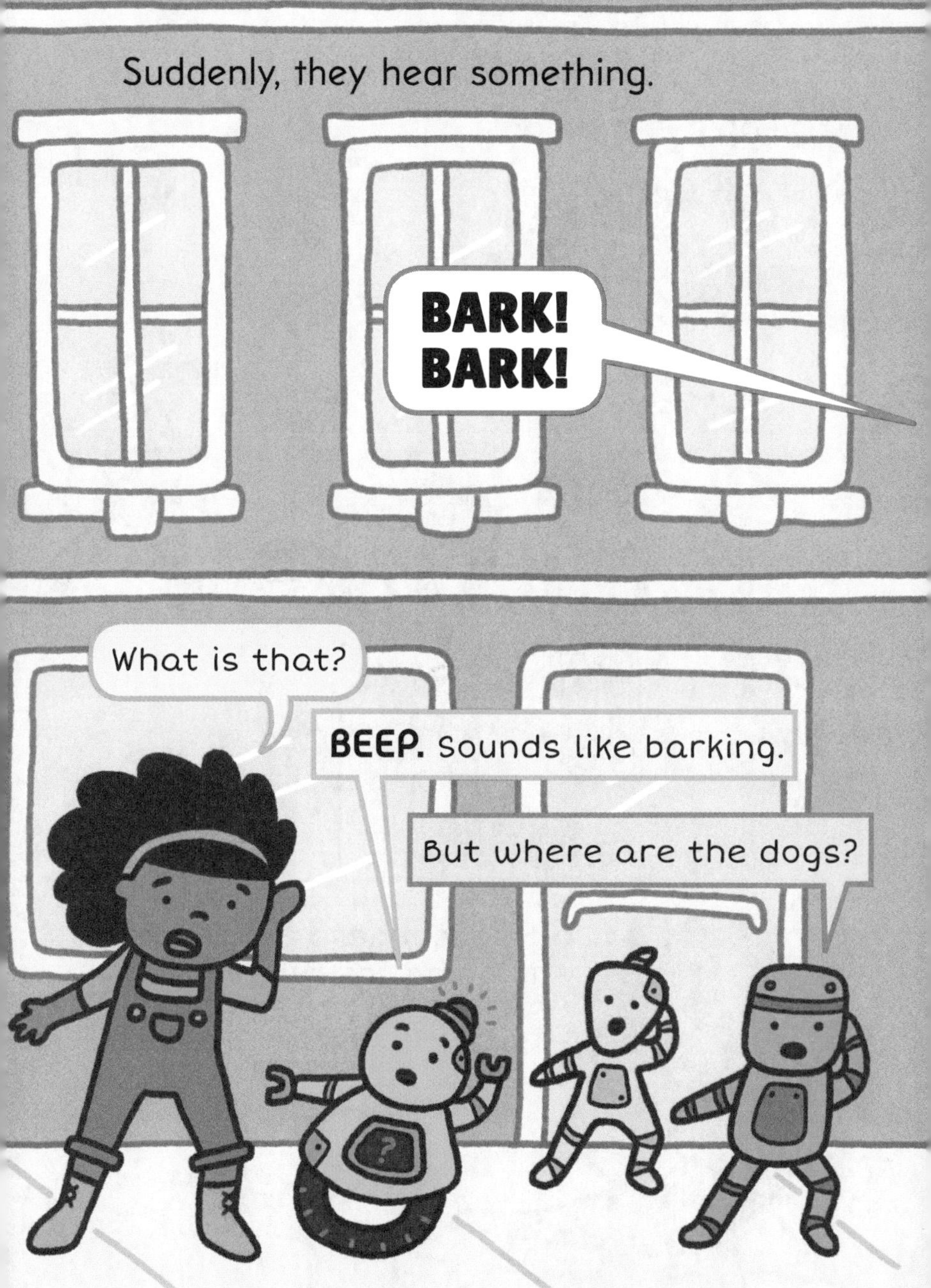
Suddenly, they hear something.
BARK! BARK!
What is that?
BEEP. Sounds like barking.
But where are the dogs?
They follow the barking sounds.

The town dog park is overflowing with people—and dogs!

So <u>this</u> is where everybody is going for fun now!

Woof-doggies!

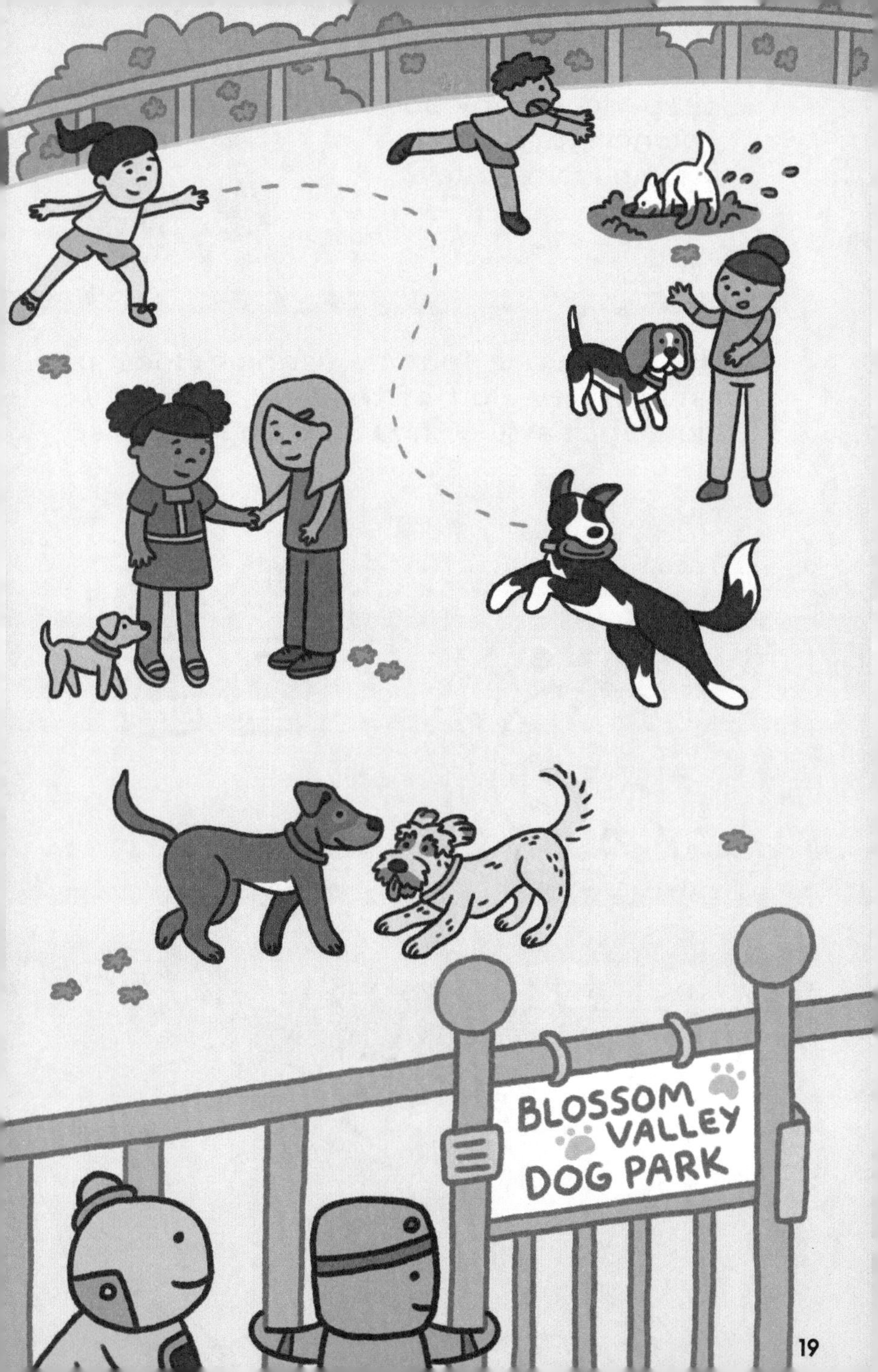
BLOSSOM
VALLEY
DOG PARK

Beep, how many dog owners are there in Blossom Valley?

BEEP. There are four thousand homes in Blossom Valley. Half of the households own a dog. That's two thousand dog owners.

Two thousand!?

Wow-zees!

Layla thinks back to when the amusement park first opened.

Happy Days used to have a doggy day care.

BEEP. That closed twelve months ago.

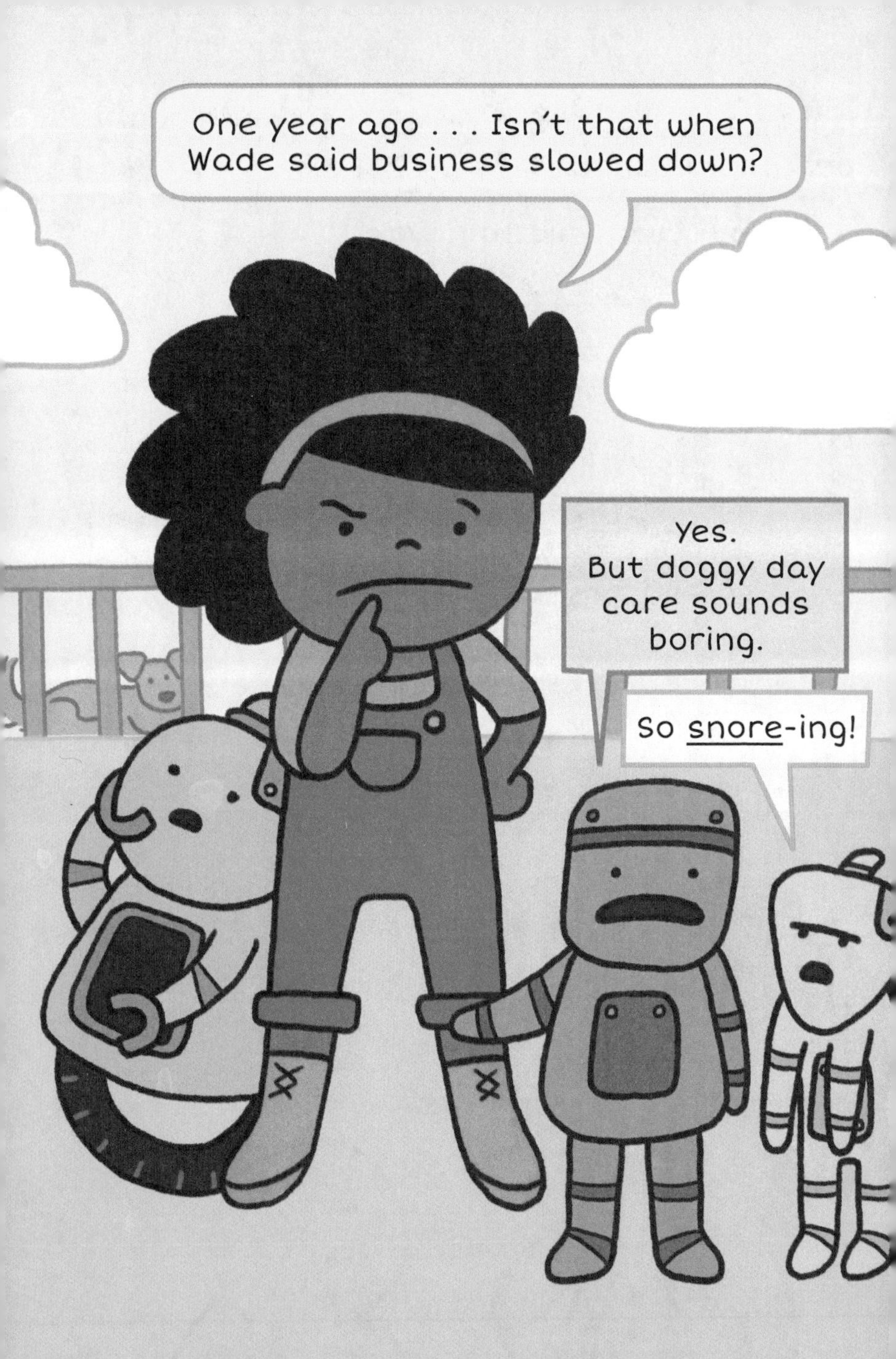
One year ago . . . Isn't that when Wade said business slowed down?
Yes. But doggy day care sounds boring.
So snore-ing!

It's true, the dogs were bored there. And the <u>whole</u> amusement park has to be fun!

This gives Layla an idea.

4
FOR THE DOGS!

Layla and the Bots rush back to Happy Days. Layla tells Wade about all the people they saw at the town dog park.

You see, people don't want to leave their dogs at home. They want to bring their dogs <u>with</u> <u>them</u> to have fun!

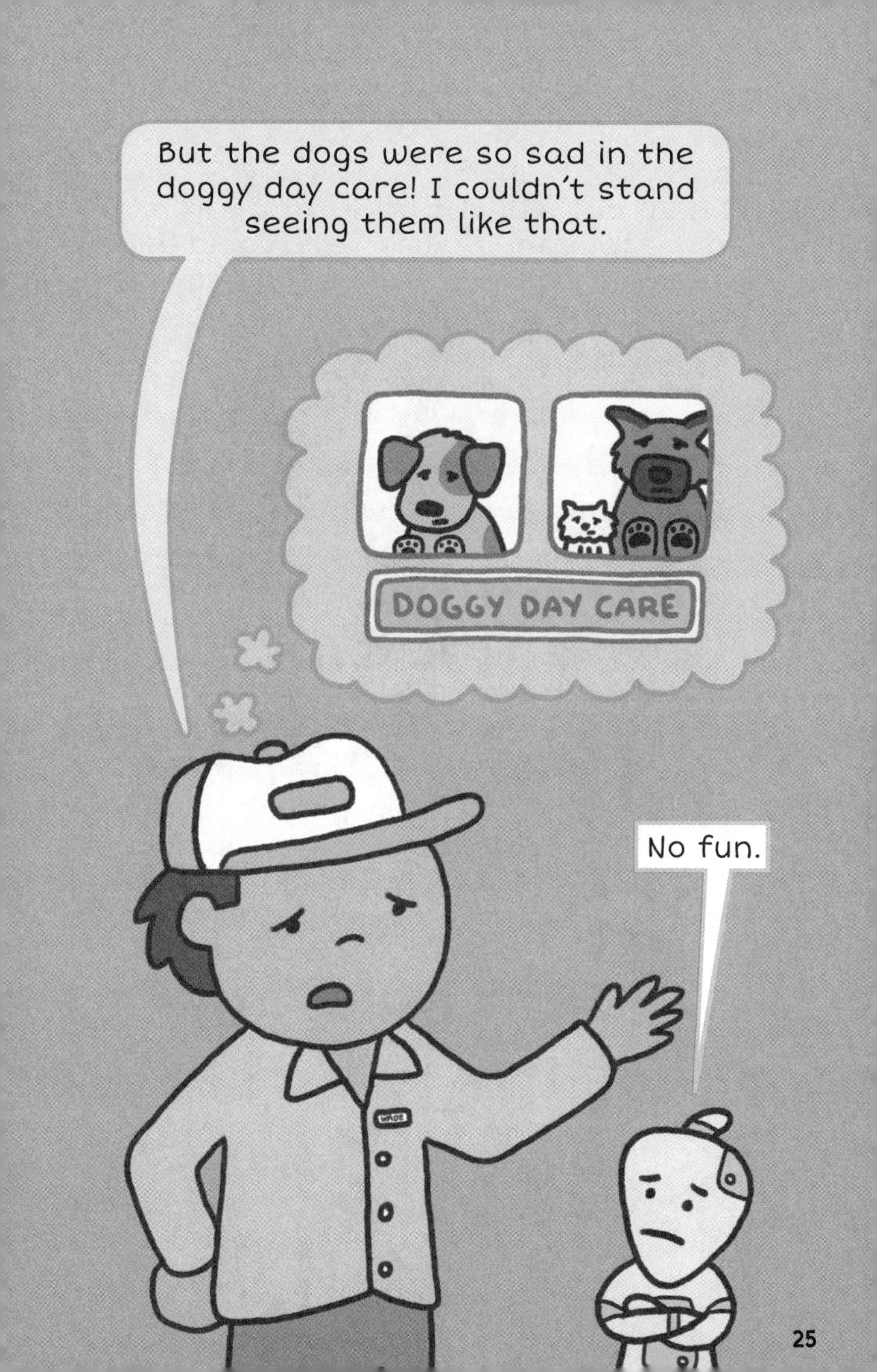
But the dogs were so sad in the doggy day care! I couldn't stand seeing them like that.
DOGGY DAY CARE
No fun.

Layla grins.

I agree! But what if Happy Days could be an amusement park that is fun for people _and_ dogs? There could be actual rides and games for <u>dogs</u>!

Wade scratches his head.

But how could we do that? We'd have to re-design the entire park. I don't think it's possible.

Layla looks at the Bots.

Layla thinks he might be right. But she has to do <u>something</u>.

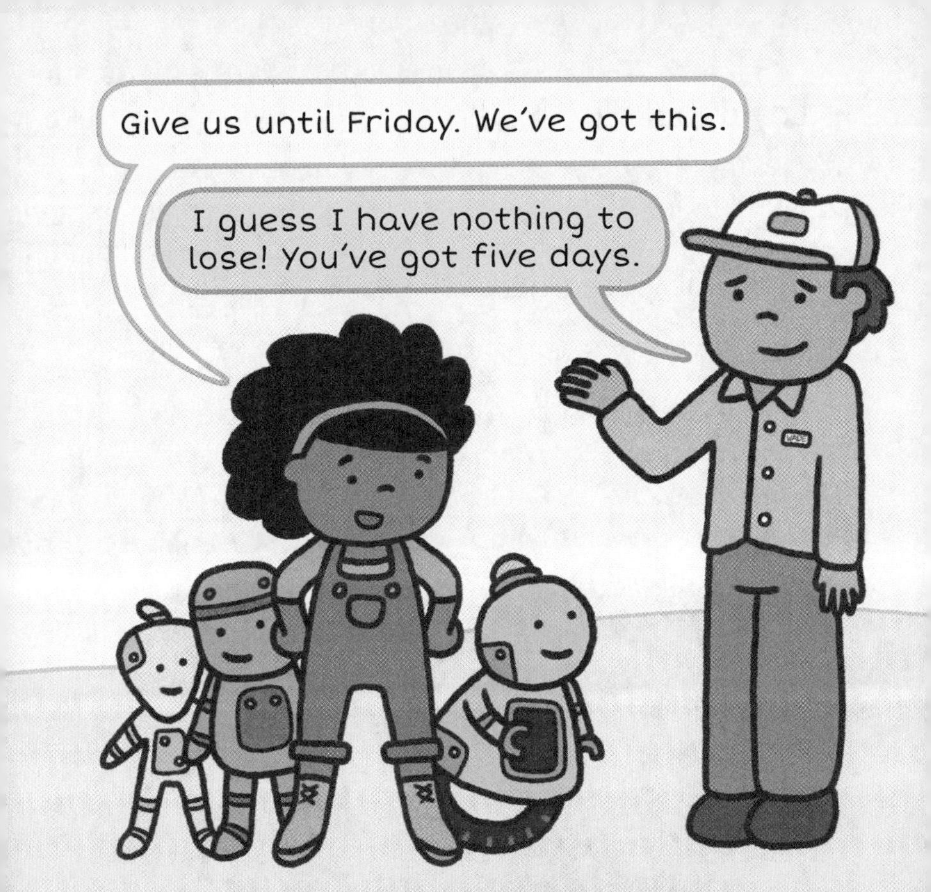
Give us until Friday. We've got this.
I guess I have nothing to lose! You've got five days.

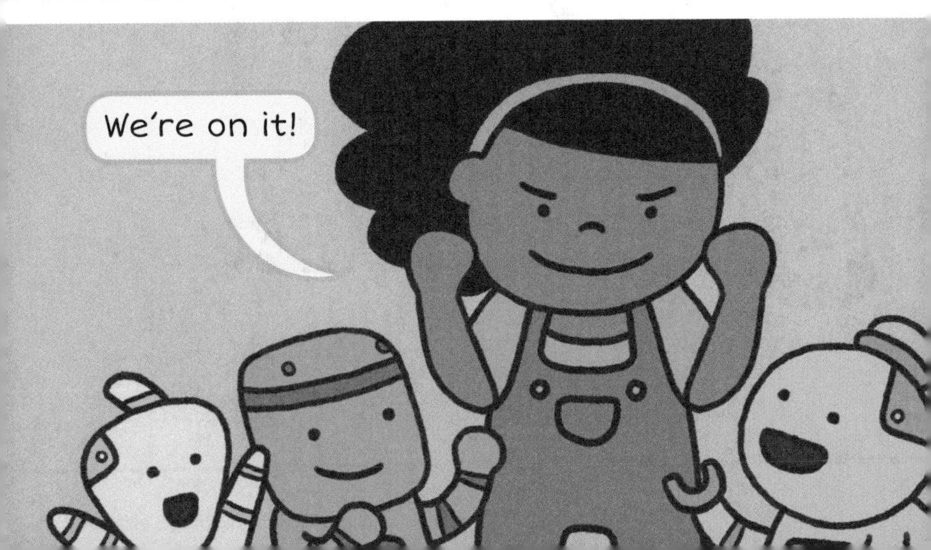
We're on it!

Inside, Layla's stomach is flipping.
Can she really do this?

5

PUPPY LOVE

The next day, Layla and the Bots sit at the ice cream shop in town. Layla has her notebook and a pencil.

Okay, Bots. We're designing an amusement park for dogs. Let me hear your ideas.

BEEP. Dog food.

Um . . . Dog collars?

Green beans!

Layla shuts her notebook.

We clearly need more information about what dogs do for fun. Follow me.

31

They head back to the dog park to
investigate some more.

They see dogs
eating treats,

dogs playing ball,

and dogs getting their
tummies rubbed.

One fluffy dog is rolling in the mud.

A brown dog is chewing on a squeaky toy.

Two spotted dogs are chasing a squirrel.

Soon, Layla is sketching ideas in her notebook. Beep, Boop, and Bop sketch too.

By the end of the day, Layla and the Bots have two dozen ideas.

BEEP. We have twenty-four ideas.

Layla squints at the mess of papers.
How is she going to choose?

6
DIAMONDS IN THE RUFF

On Wednesday morning, Layla has a plan.
She hands a stack of ideas to each Bot.

We need to get feedback on our ideas.
Let's share them with the dog owners
to hear what they think.

The dog owners love some ideas.

They don't like others.

And they make suggestions.

Layla and the Bots sit at the picnic table. Layla spreads out the winners.

We've got five great ideas! Do you think that's enough?

1 PICK-A-TREAT MACHINE!

2 TUMMY LOVE MACHINE!

3 FLYING BALL PIT!

4 RUB-A-DUB MUD SLIDE!

5 SQUEAKY TOY CHASE!

Just then, a woman with a shaggy dog runs up.

Hey, I thought of something else! My dog really loves to stick her head out the car window.

Mine too!

Same here.

Hmm . . .

Layla grabs her notebook and sketches out a new idea.

She shows the dog owners.

Yes!

Amazing!

So cool.

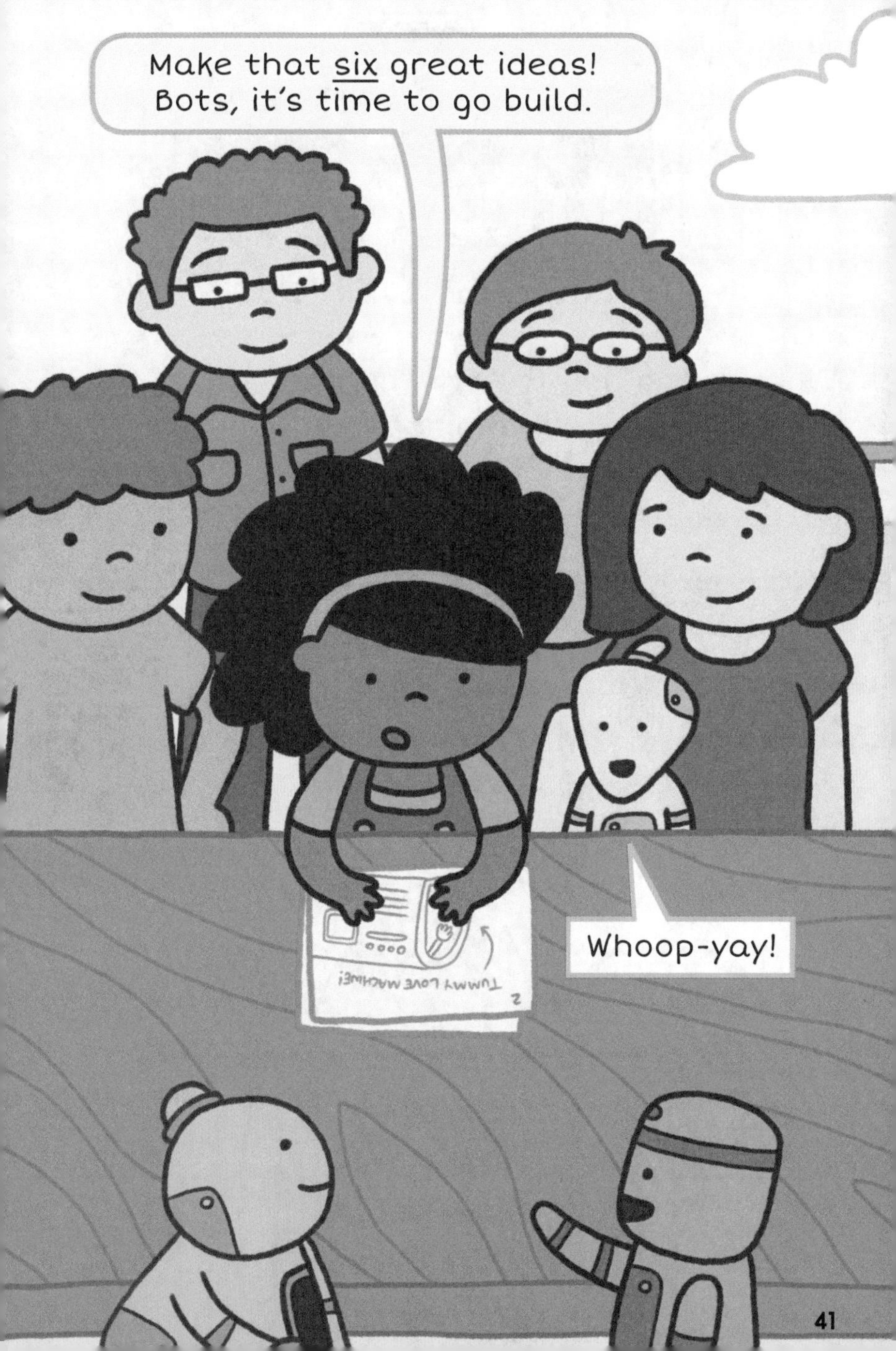
Make that six great ideas! Bots, it's time to go build.
TUMMY LOVE MACHINE!
Whoop-yay!

7
BEEP BOOP BOP

Layla and the Bots are ready to put their plan into place.

Okay, Bots, let's do this.

Beep lays out the drawings.

Boop prepares her tools.

Bop practices karate while his computers boot up.

43

First, Beep checks what dogs like to eat.

Boop builds the Pick-a-Treat machine. It is filled with bones, sausages, and doggy treats.

Bop codes the buttons to deliver the right food.

Next, Beep picks out petting styles.

Boop builds the Tummy Love machine.

It can rub,

pat,

or scratch.

Bop tinkers to get the settings just right.

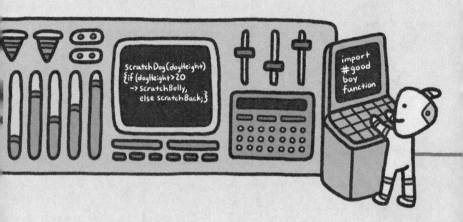

Then they build the Flying Ball Pit,

FLYING
BALL PIT

the Squeaky Toy Chase,

SQUEAKY
TOY CHASE

SQUEAK!

SQUEAK!

and the Rub-a-Dub Mud Slide.

RUB-A-DUB

MUD SLIDE

They even build a Breezy Car-Coaster!
Beep looks up all kinds of car models.

Boop builds windows
so the dogs can stick
their heads out.

Bop makes sure the cars speed up and
slow down at the right times.

TAP!
TAP!

On Thursday night, Layla and the Bots take their brand-new dog rides to Happy Days. Tomorrow they will show them to Wade.

The dogs will love this roller coaster!

LOADING DOCK

BREEZY CAR-COASTER

But as Layla lies in bed, she worries . . . Will it be enough to save the park?

8
A TOO-BIG SNAG

On Friday morning, Layla and the Bots show Wade their new inventions.

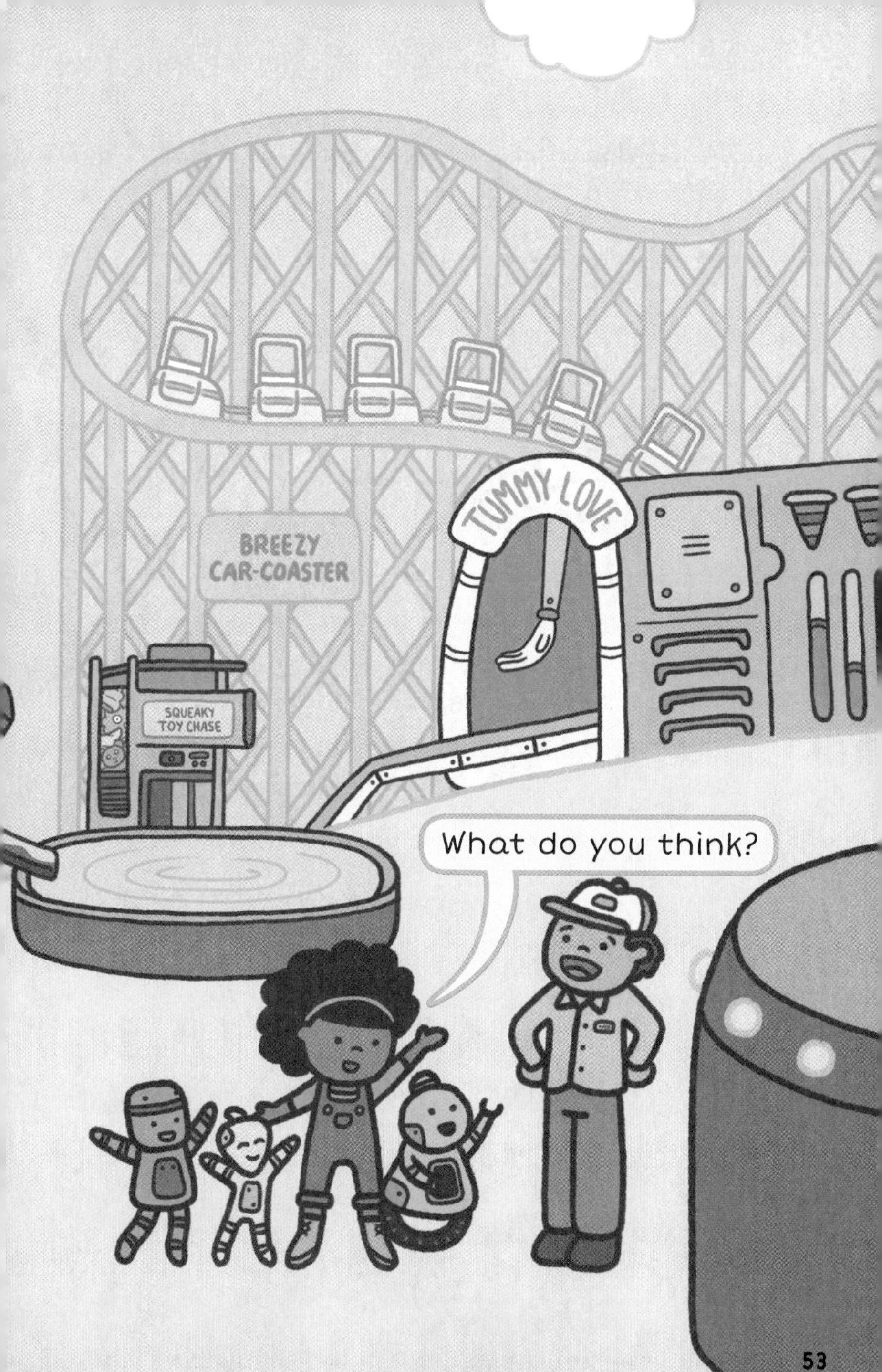
TUMMY LOVE
BREEZY CAR-COASTER
SQUEAKY TOY CHASE
What do you think?

Layla, these rides are amazing!

Layla glows.

I'll call the safety inspector. She'll need to approve the new rides.

Go get ready for your show. We will re-open the park this afternoon!

Layla and the Bots dance their way toward the stage.

See you at the show!

They start tuning their instruments. But then . . .

Wade runs over to them.
He looks worried.

We've got a problem. The safety inspector won't approve the Breezy Car-Coaster. She says the windows are too big and a small dog could fall out.

Too big?

Uh-ohs!

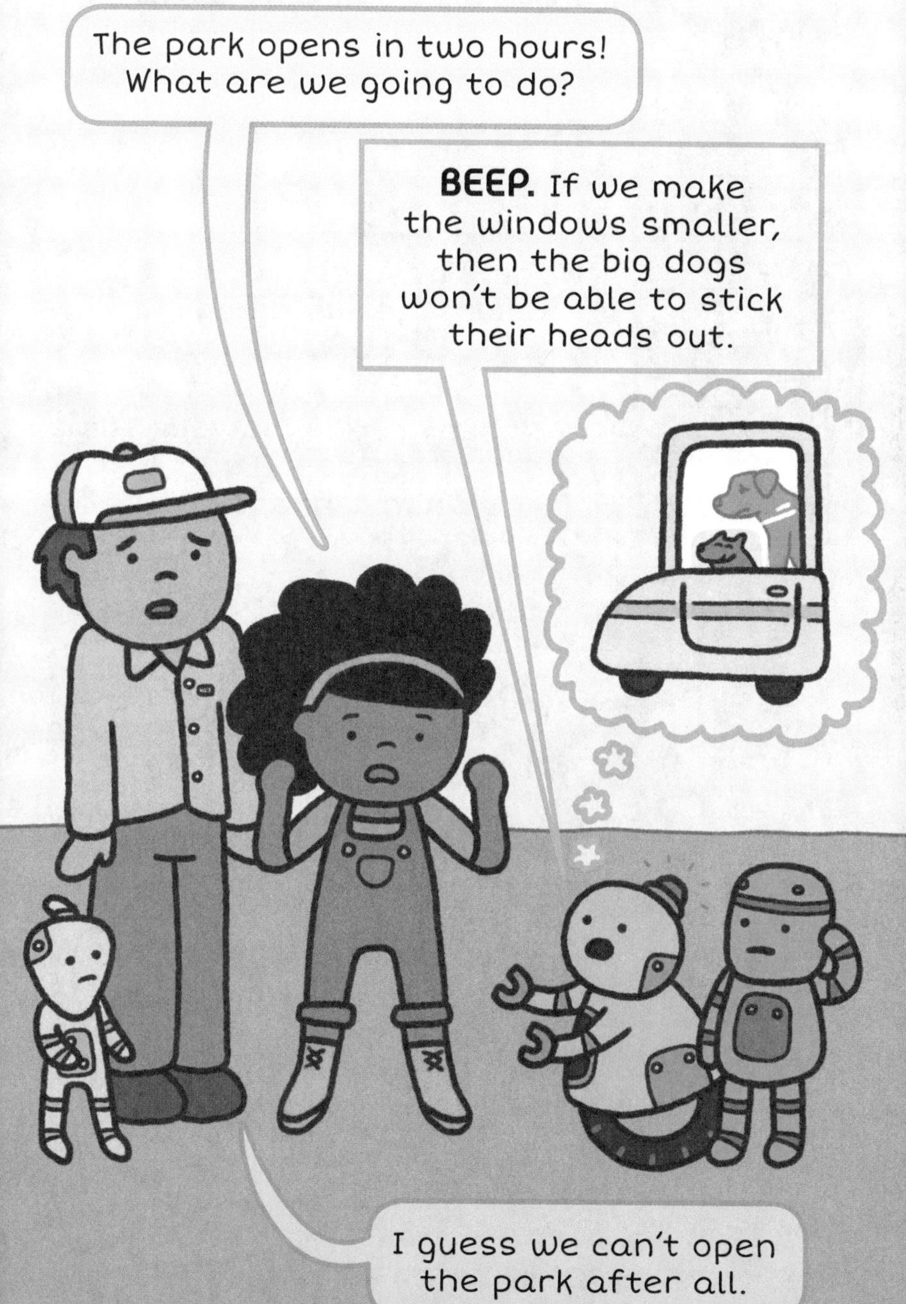
The park opens in two hours! What are we going to do?
BEEP. If we make the windows smaller, then the big dogs won't be able to stick their heads out.
I guess we can't open the park after all.

Layla slumps down on the edge of the stage.

Wade, I'm so sorry I let you down. I let us <u>all</u> down.

No, Layla. You did your best. Maybe Happy Paws just wasn't meant to be.

BEEP. This challenge was just too big.

Yep, wrong size!

Suddenly, Layla looks up.

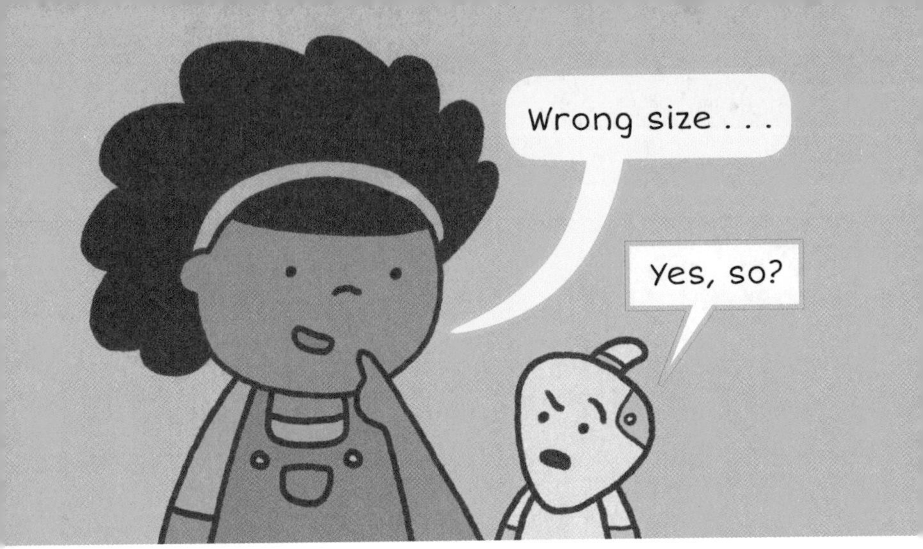
Wrong size . . .
Yes, so?

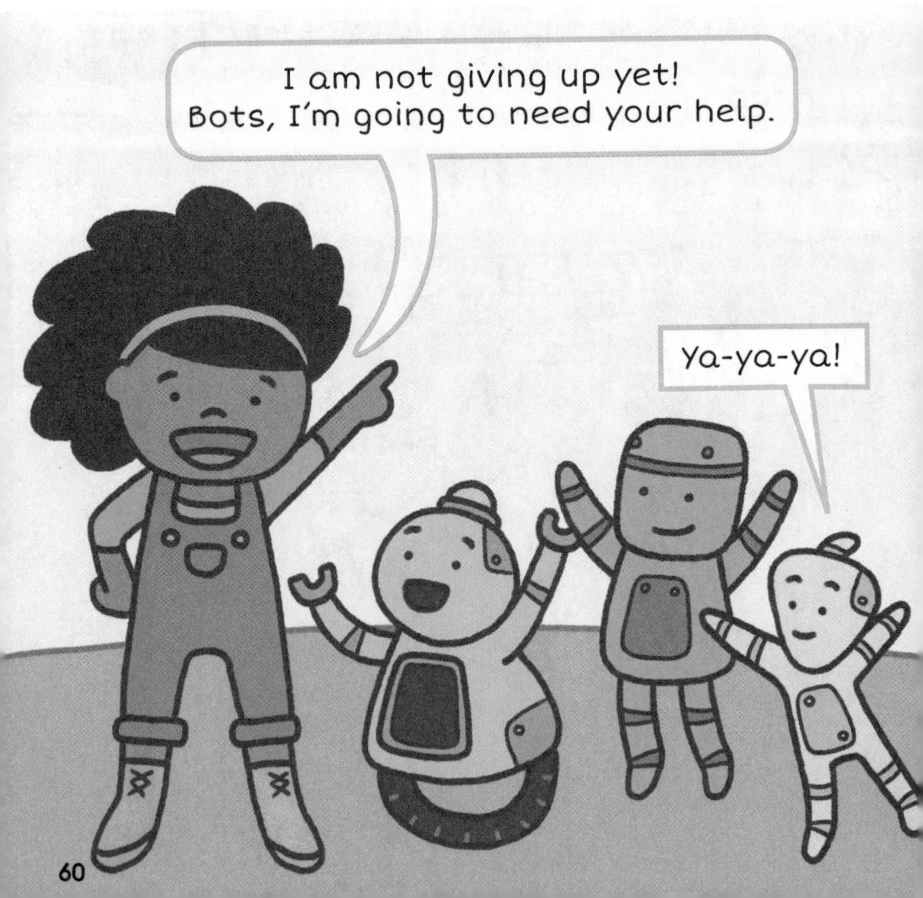
I am not giving up yet!
Bots, I'm going to need your help.
Ya-ya-ya!

Beep, get me sizes for all kinds of dogs. I want to know small and large sizes.

BEEP!
Okay!

Boop, add a camera to the loading dock.

But why?

Just trust me!

And Bop, you come with me. We've got less than two hours until the park opens!

Layla and the Bots work together until the Breezy Car-Coaster is fixed.

9

BEST IN SHOW

The safety inspector looks over the new Breezy Car-Coaster.

63

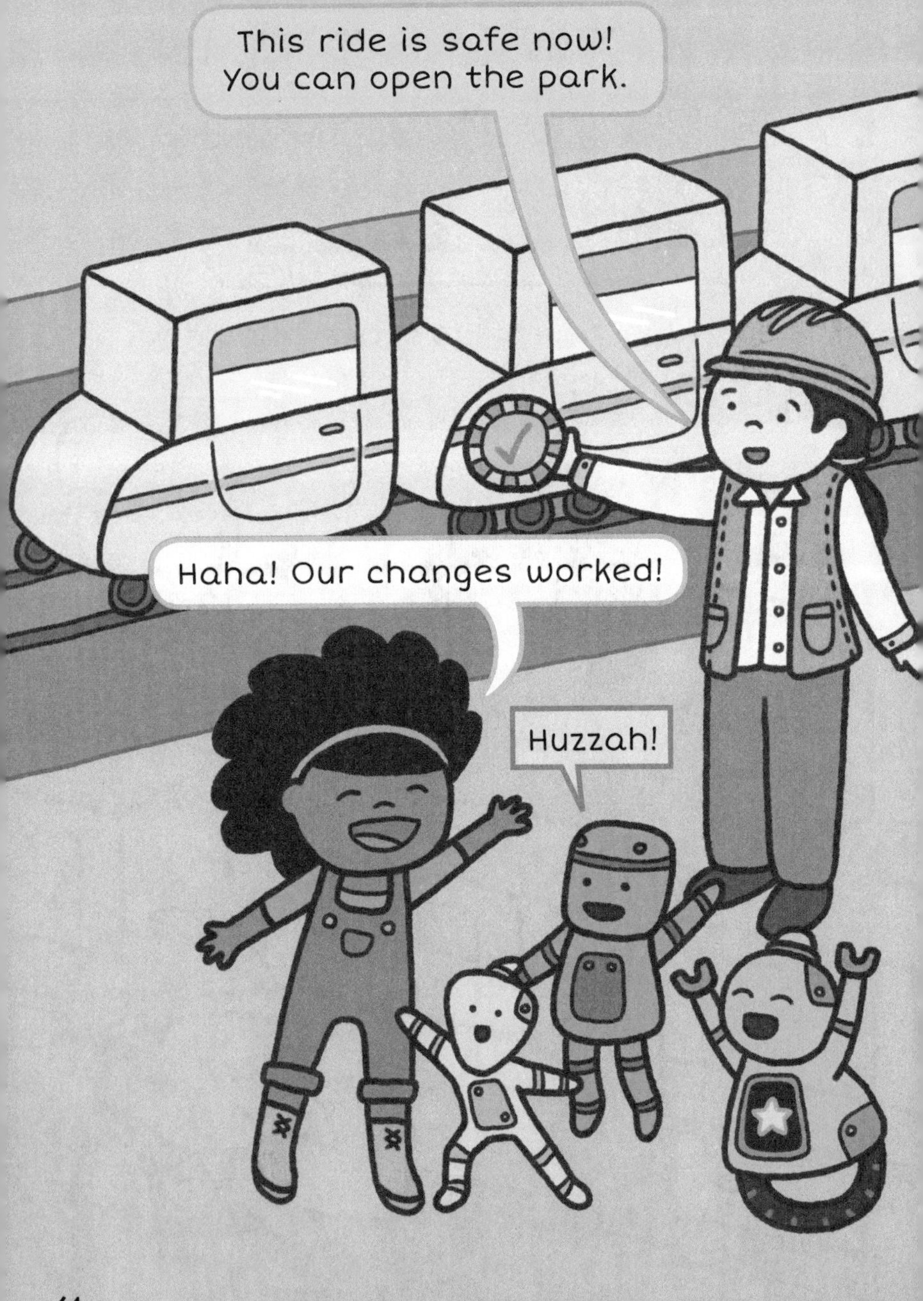
This ride is safe now! You can open the park.
Haha! Our changes worked!
Huzzah!

Wow, I can't believe it. How did you fix the Car-Coaster?

Easy. Bop and I wrote code to change the size of the window. Let me show you what I mean.

Layla shows Wade the updated plans for the Breezy Car-Coaster.

BREEZY CAR-COASTER

When a dog steps up to the loading dock, the camera measures its size.

CAMERA

Then the code adjusts how far the window opens.

If small dog -> window up high
If medium dog -> window half open
If big dog -> window down low

For small dogs, the window is small. For big dogs, the window is big.

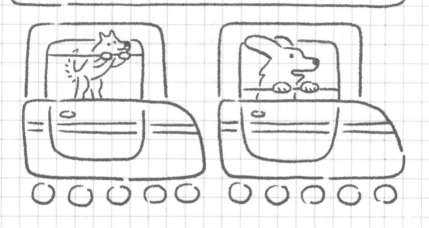

This way, the window is the perfect size for each dog that enters the ride.

Wade high-fives Layla.

It's genius!

Thanks, Wade.

Thank <u>you</u>, Layla and the Bots! You saved the park! You rock.

That's right! We <u>do</u> rock!

Wade opens the park. Everyone loves Happy Paws!

Soon, it's time to rock out!

It was Layla and the Bots' best show ever.

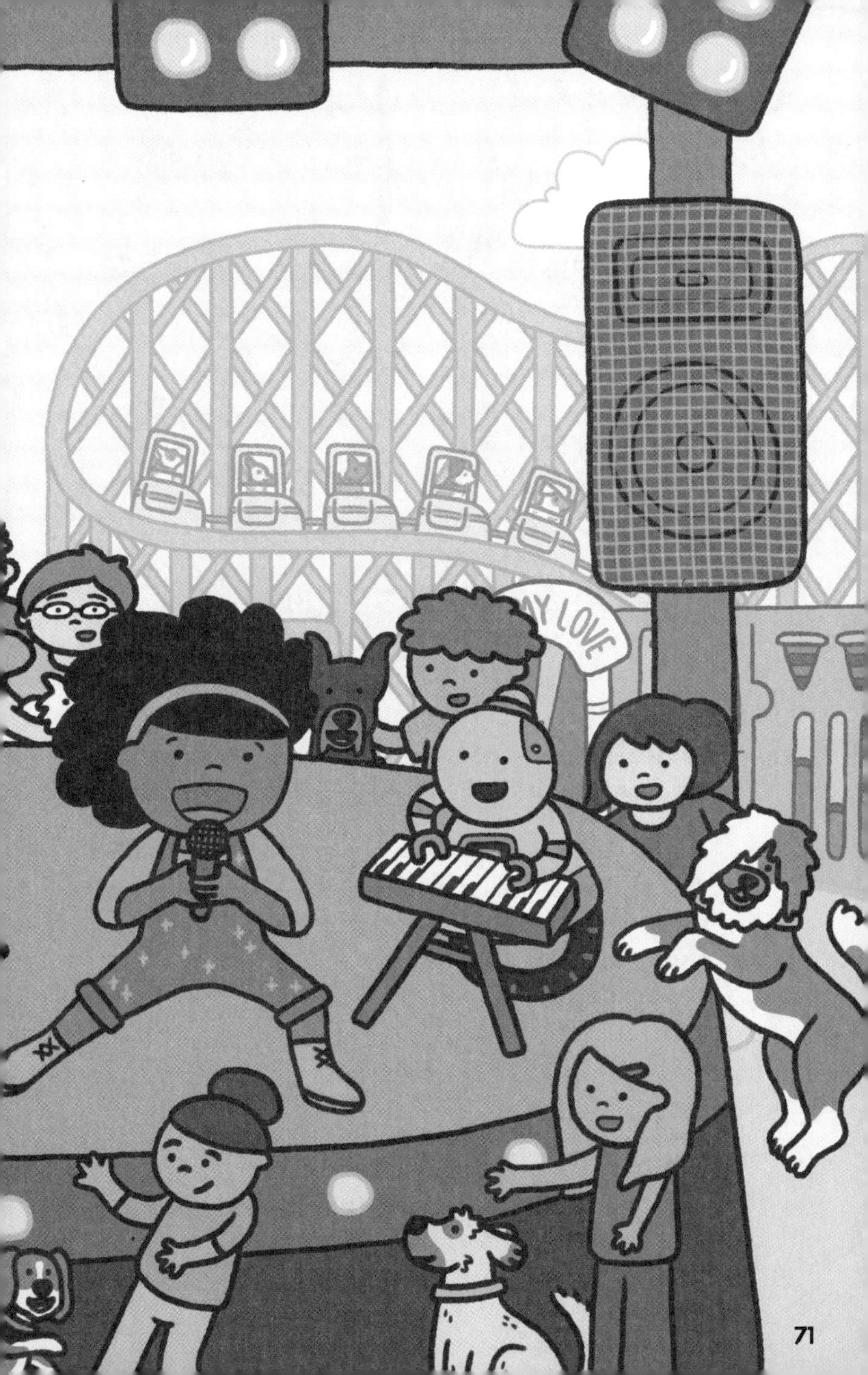
MY LOVE

DESIGN AND BUILD YOUR OWN

YOU'LL NEED THE FOLLOWING ITEMS:

- 5 or more cardboard tubes
- 5 or more plastic bottles
- 1 large piece of cardboard
- Scissors
- Glue
- Duct tape
- Marble or small ball
- Paper cup (optional)

NOTE: Many of these items can come from your recycling bin! Be sure to have an adult clean out the bottles and remove any staples from the cardboard.

STEP 1. BUILD THE BASE

- Tape the bottles to your cardboard base. These are the pillars for your roller coaster.

TIP: Line up your pillars from tallest to shortest. Keep them close enough that your cardboard tubes can connect them.

STEP 2. BUILD THE TRACK

- Cut your cardboard tubes in half length-wise to create pieces for your track.
- Place your tracks to connect the pillars and tape them into place.

ROLLER COASTER!

STEP 3. TEST AND FIX

- Test out your roller coaster! Place your marble at the top and watch it zoom down the track.

- Does your marble fall off? Or get stuck? It's time to problem solve! Add, move, or take away from your design to make it work.

TIP: You can add a cup to the end of the track to catch your ball.

STEP 4. ROCK OUT!

- Have fun! Experiment with different-sized balls, track designs, and pillar heights to see what happens.

- Give your ride a fun name, and draw a picture of your design.

- Decorate your roller coaster with paint, glitter, and anything else you'd like!

HOW MUCH DO YOU KNOW ABOUT HAPPY PAWS?

Reread page 11. How does Layla feel when Wade tells her that Happy Days has to close? How do you know she feels this way?

Happy Days used to have a doggy day care, but it closed. What happened to the park <u>after</u> the doggy day care closed?

Layla and the Bots visit the dog park to learn what dogs do for fun. What do they see at the park? What ideas come out of this visit?

The safety inspector won't approve the Breezy Car-Coaster. What problem did she find? How do Layla and the Bots fix the problem?

Imagine you get to build an amusement park for pets! What animals would visit your park? What rides would you make for them? Draw and label a map of your park!

ABOUT THE CREATORS

VICKY FANG is a product designer who invents things like cars that talk to each other and robots you can build at home. She has never designed a roller coaster for dogs, but she did help her boys design a terrarium for their pet darkling beetle! Vicky lives in California with her husband and kids. LAYLA AND THE BOTS is her first early chapter book series.

CHRISTINE NISHIYAMA
is an artist who draws all kinds of things in her sketchbook. She's passionate about helping others make art and teaches students
online. Christine lives in North Carolina with her husband and her dog, Oni. Christine is also the author and illustrator of the picture book WE ARE FUNGI.

READ MORE

LAYLA and the BOTS

BOOKS!

LAYLA and the BOTS
HAPPY PAWS
written by Vicky Fang
illustrated by Christine Nishiyama
SCHOLASTIC
1

LAYLA and the BOTS
BUILT FOR SPEED
written by Vicky Fang
illustrated by Christine Nishiyama
SCHOLASTIC
2

LAYLA and the BOTS
CUPCAKE FIX
written by Vicky Fang
illustrated by Christine Nishiyama
SCHOLASTIC
3

LAYLA and the BOTS
MAKING WAVES
written by Vicky Fang
illustrated by Christine Nishiyama
SCHOLASTIC
4